To my husband John, who is my EVERYDAY SUPERHERO, and all other EVERYDAY HEROES.

- Denise L. Kaminsky

www.mascotbooks.com

Nittany Lion™ Everyday Superhero

For more information, please contact:
Mascot Books
620 Herndon Parkway #320
Herndon, VA 20170
info@mascotbooks.com

CPSIA Code: PRT0618A
ISBN-13: 978-1-68401-914-4

Printed in the United States

NITTANY LION™
EVERYDAY SUPERHERO

Denise L. Kaminsky '73

Illustrated by

Michelle Brownlow '92

Early one morning on the Penn State Campus, Nittany Lion yawned, stretched, and hopped out of bed. He began his morning exercises with push-ups. Being strong was important.

While eating breakfast, Nittany Lion saw his stack of library books. *Today, I get to help the librarian as the substitute reader for Story Hour,* thought Nittany Lion. *I must take a quick shower, brush my teeth, and make my bed.*

Nittany Lion picked up his library books and headed to the library. *I can't be late!* he thought. *I know, I'll ride the bus and be there in no time.*

On the way to the bus stop, Nittany Lion saw some visitors looking at a Penn State Campus map. They were talking about the Berkey Creamery.

"Hello, do you need some help?" he asked.

"WOW! It's the Nittany Lion. We're trying to find the Creamery, do you know where it is?" asked the boy.

It took Nittany Lion only a few seconds to show them where to get some delicious ice cream.

He continued on to the bus stop. But when he got there, he saw the bus leaving.

I'll just keep walking, thought Nittany Lion. *If I hurry, I won't be late.*

Along the way, Nittany Lion spotted a car with a flat tire. A man was looking in the trunk. "Do you need some help?" he asked.

"I do need help. I can't find my jack to lift the car," the man said.

"No problem. I can lift the car while you change the tire," offered Nittany Lion.

"Great!"

The tire was changed quickly.

"Thank you, Nittany Lion. I couldn't have done it without you," said the man.

"You're welcome," said Nittany Lion, waving goodbye.

If I jog to the library I won't be late, thought Nittany Lion.

Around the corner, Nittany Lion spotted some children putting up a sign. The sign read, "Lost Kitty."

"Do you need some help?" asked Nittany Lion.

"Yes, we're trying to find my kitty. Can you please help?" asked the little girl.

"Let me think. I know just where cats like to go," he said, looking up in a tree.

"Not in that one."

He looked up into another tree and saw the missing kitten sitting on a high branch.

Nittany Lion climbed up and then gently carried it down. He placed the kitten in the little girl's arms.

"You saved my kitty! You're the best, Nittany Lion," she said as her friends clapped and cheered.

Nittany Lion wiggled his ears, smiled, and jogged away.

Right on time, Nittany Lion jogged in to the Children's Room of the library. He gave out some high fives to the waiting children. Nittany Lion loved reading to them about the United States, famous people, sports, animals, the environment, and all kinds of things. He liked to read a lot.

"Hello, Nittany Lion," said Mrs. Rivera, the librarian. "The children are ready to listen!"

"Great!" said Nittany Lion, sitting down in the Reader's Chair. "Today, I want to read to you about a famous young person. He was not much older than you, and he was a hero. What makes someone a hero?"

"Someone who is brave," answered Brianna.

"Someone who is smart," called Ben and Raj.

Nittany Lion wiggled his ears. "Yes! A hero is someone who does something special to help others."

"Louis Braille was a blind teenager who lived in France in the mid 1800s. He loved books, but he couldn't see to read. So Louis invented raised dots on a page that a blind person can 'read' with his or her fingers. See the dots in my book? You can touch them if you like."

"WOW!" said the children.

"Once a blind person learned what letters the dots made, he or she could read just like us," explained Nittany Lion. "Louis was a hero because he helped blind people read."

"My uncle makes new legs for people. Is he a hero?" asked Jaxxon.

"Yes," said Nittany Lion.

"My grandma takes care of me sometimes. She is my hero," said Jenna.

Nittany Lion smiled and wiggled his ears. "We all can be heroes in our own special way. Thank you for being good listeners."

The children clapped.

Mrs. Rivera said, "Nittany Lion, you are a hero to me. You always come when I need you to read to the children. I know you help others every day as well. I have something for you." She opened a bag and pulled out something blue. It was a cape! She tied it around Nittany Lion's neck. "Thank you for all you do every day. You are an Everyday Superhero to all of us."

Nittany Lion whirled around, wiggled his ears, and roared.

ROAR!

Nittany Lion headed outside. Nearby, he saw the janitor on a tall ladder changing a light bulb. The janitor reached a little too far and started falling off the ladder. Nittany Lion ran over and caught him!

"Thank you, Nittany Lion!" said the janitor. "You saved me! You really are an Everyday Superhero."

Nittany Lion put down the janitor and ROARED!

About the Author

Denise graduated from Penn State ('73 EKED) and then received a MS in Reading from SUNY. She was a reading specialist and a third grade teacher. Denise is the author of *Nittany Lion Has the Hiccups*, *Nittany Lion Gets a Big Surprise*, *Nittany Lion Tells the Legend of Princess Nit-a-Nee*, *Nittany Lion's Pennsylvania Vacation*, *Nittany Lion and THON*, and *Nittany Lion and Earth Day*. She is the mother of two grown children, Jessie and Jay. Currently, she lives in Happy Valley with her husband, John. They are big Penn State fans.

About the Illustrator

Michelle graduated from Penn State in 1992 (Arts & Architecture, Sigma Kappa). Formerly a middle school and high school art teacher in upstate New York, she now writes young adult and new adult novels from her home town in Pennsylvania. Not only did she meet her husband at Penn State, but their two oldest children, Matthew and Emily, are currently students at Main Campus. Izaiah, their youngest, has more than a couple years to figure out where he wants to go. WE ARE...

Have a book idea?

Contact us at:

info@mascotbooks.com | www.mascotbooks.com